The Huffalots

Eve Coy

Andersen Press

A mother is waking up her Huffalots.

They are very strange creatures...

In the morning they wake up… GRUMPY.
They are irritable and tired.
Nothing is right for them.

They don't want to
get up or stay in bed.

They don't like
their clothes

but they don't want to
wear their pyjamas…

And they don't

like each other.

Then it's breakfast time.

They like the same cup,   they don't like

the same food.

But as they eat their breakfast
the first magical transformation
occurs and…

... they become Huffalittles.
Now, Huffalittles are different from Huffalots.

They still don't
like their clothes,

though their dinosaur
jumpers are OK,

but they won't
wear their coats!

They quite like to race

and to chase around the park.

Every day, one of the Huffalittles will
trip over. The other Huffalittle will
give them a great big hug,

and sometimes
a feather,

or a flower.

And it's around this time
that the second magical
transformation occurs...

... they become Lovealittles.
Lovealittles are different from Huffalittles.

They tend to be
a bit happier.
They still like to chase,

but also give
each other blossom
and sticks...

... and lovely cuddles.

It's around this time that the third magical transformation occurs...

... and they become Lovealots.
Lovealots are different
from Lovealittles.

At home the Lovealots are busy.

Now everything is funny, particularly each other,

and everything is lovely, particularly each other.

But with supper, jobs, noise and mess,
it's often around this time that Mum
becomes... a Huffalot.

She is grumpy.

She is irritable.

She is tired.

Nothing is right for her.

But the Lovealots know just what to do.

They give her a
picture of a feather,

and a paper flower,

and a great big hug.

Which means she stops
being a Huffalot.

And then
with suds

and bubbles…

... and the greatest of cuddles,
all are Lovealots once more.

Snuggled up with a story
as another day ends,
one thing is clear,

whether Huffalot or Lovealot,
they each know they're
loved a lot.